# Dear Parent:

Congratulations! Your child is taking the first steps on an exciting journey. The destination? Independent reading!

**STEP INTO READING®** will help your child get there. The program offers five steps to reading success. Each step includes fun stories and colorful art. There are also Step into Reading Sticker Books, Step into Reading Math Readers, Step into Reading Phonics Readers, Step into Reading Write-In Readers, and Step into Reading Phonics Boxed Sets—a complete literacy program with something for every child.

## Learning to Read, Step by Step!

### Ready to Read   Preschool–Kindergarten
• big type and easy words • rhyme and rhythm • picture clues
For children who know the alphabet and are eager to begin reading.

### Reading with Help   Preschool–Grade 1
• basic vocabulary • short sentences • simple stories
For children who recognize familiar words and sound out new words with help.

### Reading on Your Own   Grades 1–3
• engaging characters • easy-to-follow plots • popular topics
For children who are ready to read on their own.

### Reading Paragraphs   Grades 2–3
• challenging vocabulary • short paragraphs • exciting stories
For newly independent readers who read simple sentences with confidence.

### Ready for Chapters   Grades 2–4
• chapters • longer paragraphs • full-color art
For children who want to take the plunge into chapter books but still like colorful pictures.

**STEP INTO READING®** is designed to give every child a successful reading experience. The grade levels are only guides. Children can progress through the steps at their own speed, developing confidence in their reading, no matter what their grade.

Remember, a lifetime love of reading starts with a single step!

*For my friends at Annie Bloom's Books*
*—J.L.W*

Visit us on the Web!
StepIntoReading.com
randomhouse.com/kids

Educators and librarians, for a variety of teaching tools, visit us at RHTeachersLibrarians.com

ISBN: 978-0-7364-3013-5 (trade) — ISBN: 978-0-7364-8120-5 (lib. bdg.)

Printed in the United States of America    10 9 8 7 6

# STEP INTO READING®

STEP 1

## DISNEY PRINCESS

# Princess Hearts

By Jennifer Liberts Weinberg

Illustrated by Francesco Legramandi

Random House 🏠 New York

Valentine's Day
at the castle
is fun!

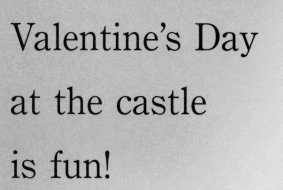

Cinderella
gives hugs
to everyone.

Rapunzel's gift
is tied in a bow.

A Valentine heart
makes the sky glow.

Red roses for Aurora
are so sweet!

A Valentine kiss
is always a treat.

Belle's love stories
are red, pink,
and white.

Valentine cupcakes

make a yummy sight!

Seven sweet
valentines
stand in line.

Snow White asks
her friends,
"Will you be mine?"

Jasmine has
Valentine candies
to share.

24

Ariel's gift
looks great
in her hair.

A Valentine parade
feels just right.

Tiana and her prince
dance all night.

# Happy Valentine's Day!